Lucas
With Love from
Great Grandma
Barb

HALLOWEEN CIRCUS

By Charise Neugebauer

Illustrated by Robert Ingpen

A Michael Neugebauer Book · NORTH-SOUTH BOOKS
New York / London

Fold out front endpaper poster

Doors lock. Owls hoot.

Bat wings thump. Fat rats scoot.

Shadows crawl. Nightmares creep.

Fires burn. Graveyards weep.

Ghosts will fly north and east.

A celebration for the best of beasts.

South and west, bones move slow.

Tombstones call to all who know.

A black cat stares an evil smile.

A small child dreams for a little while.

The fog rolls in. The child is gone.

There's a Halloween circus
    at the graveyard lawn.

Thunder chants. The spirits feast.

Drummers tap their measured beat.

Trumpets sound. They all march in.

Center stage. The show begins.

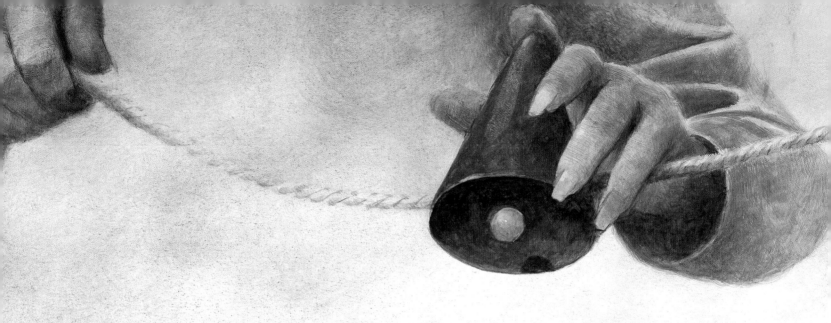

Crusty newts and haunting vapors.

Flickering lights and funny capers.

Abra-ca-dab-bra. Dab-bra-ca-doo.

I'll change you into something new!

Lost souls. Shaken bones.

Witches' games. Magic cones.

Follow me right through the air.

Without a tightrope if you dare!

Fold out back endpaper poster ➜

Invisible feet and silent sounds.

Halloween treats and sweets abound.

Soft as shadows and green as goo.

Cotton candy just for you!

Hocus-pocus. Round and round.

Red as blood is a scary sound.

Blazing candles. A pumpkin's grin.

Familiar faces once again!

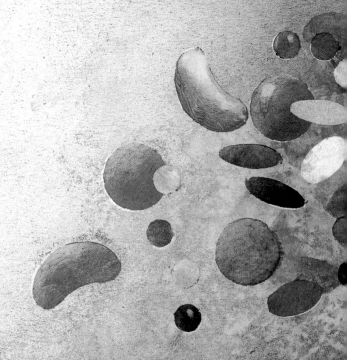

Spooky surprises here and there.

What you see in here, is where?

First you see it. Now you don't.

What you think you'll see, you won't!

Dragon air and butterfly wings.

Twist and turn, many more things.

Twist this way, a witch's broom.

Twist once more and watch it zoom!

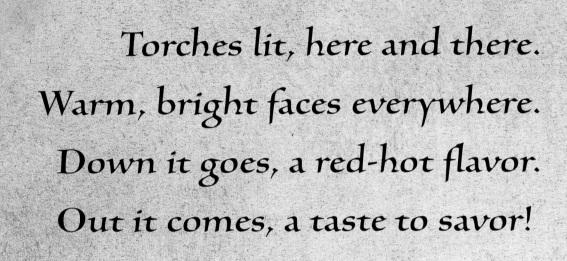

Torches lit, here and there.
Warm, bright faces everywhere.
Down it goes, a red-hot flavor.
Out it comes, a taste to savor!

The sun is rising. Our fun must fade.
But we will return for next year's parade.
You've been a great guest
from midnight to dawn
for our Halloween circus
at the graveyard lawn!

So until we meet again next year,

Think of us without fear.

Ghosts are dreams. We're nothing more.

And without your dreams, life is such a bore!

So dream a dream while you're awake.

Be where you want. See what you make.

And all night long and in between,

Dream sweet dreams of Halloween!

Copyright © 2002 by Michael Neugebauer Verlag, an imprint of
Nord-Süd Verlag AG, Gossau Zürich, Switzerland
First published in Switzerland under the title HALLOWEEN NACHT.

First published in Great Britain in 2002 by North-South Books,
an imprint of Nord-Süd Verlag AG, Gossau Zürich, Switzerland.
First published in the United States, Canada, Australia, and New Zealand in 2003
by North-South Books, an imprint of Nord-Süd Verlag AG, Gossau Zürich,
Switzerland.

Distributed in the United States by North-South Books Inc., New York.

Library of Congress Cataloging-in-Publication Data is available.
A CIP catalogue record for this book is available from The British Library.
ISBN 0-7358-1683-2 (trade edition) 10 9 8 7 6 5 4 3 2 1
Printed in Italy

For more information about our books, and the authors and artists
who create them, visit our web site: www.northsouth.com